This book belongs to:

This 1989 Muppet Press book is published by Longmeadow Press.
Distributed by Checkerboard Press. a division of Macmillan, Inc.

Printed in U.S.A.
ISBN 002-689370-3
h g f e d c b a

The Fraggles
Over, Under, and Between

by Laurie Berns illustrated by Larry Di Fiori

Muppet Press

One day as I lay dreaming
Beside a mossy tree,
A Fraggle I knew very well
Came bouncing up to me.
I thought I heard her calling
As off she quickly ran,
"Oh, wake up, Mokey Fraggle—
And catch me if you can!"

She scampered **up** a ladder
That stood in Lonesome Cave.
I scampered right **up** after her—
I thought I was so brave.

She shimmied **down** a long, long rope—
I heard her distant laughter.
I took a deep breath, held on tight,
And **down** I shimmied after.

I chased her to a canyon—
It was so deep and wide.
As I ran **in**, my friend was climbing
Out the other side.

I found a little shortcut,
And quickly I crawled **through** it.
"Hurry up!" she called to me.
"I know that you can do it."

She led me up a mountainside
Where wild patoozies grow.
Then I looked down and saw her
In the valley far **below**.

Down I skipped in search of her—
I thought I heard her call.
When I looked up, I saw her
Right **above** a waterfall.

I swam **across** a river;
I swam **between** some rocks.
But all I saw was Boober,
Wringing out some socks.

I came upon a little house,
All decorated sweetly.
It had a funny little fence,
Which I climbed **over** neatly.

I peered **around** the open door
And saw a little chair.
It was so tiny that I thought,
She can't be **under** there!

I looked **beneath** the little bed;

I looked **behind** the chest.

I peered **into** a bag of beans—
I really did my best.

But when I found this giant box,
I had to rub my eyes.
And when I finally opened it,
I got one big…

SURPRISE!

And when the day was over,
I thought of all I'd done.
With **over**, **under**, **up**, and **through**,
I'd had a lot of fun!